MAX AND RUBY'S
·MIDAS·

ANOTHER GREEK MYTH

ROSEMARY WELLS

DIAL BOOKS FOR YOUNG READERS · NEW YORK

*   *For Amy and Cynthia Glidden*   *

Published by Dial Books for Young Readers
A Division of Penguin Books USA Inc.
375 Hudson Street
New York, New York 10014

Typography by Jane Byers Bierhorst
Printed in the U.S.A.
First Edition
1 3 5 7 9 10 8 6 4 2

Library of Congress Cataloging in Publication Data
Wells, Rosemary.
Max and Ruby's Midas : another Greek myth / Rosemary Wells.
p.   cm.
Summary: Ruby tries to stop her younger brother Max from eating
so many sweets by reading him an altered
version of the story of King Midas.
ISBN 0-8037-1782-2. — ISBN 0-8037-1783-0 (lib. bdg.)
[1. Food habits — Fiction.   2. Brothers and sisters — Fiction.
3. Rabbits — Fiction.]   I. Title.   II. Title: Midas.
PZ7.W46843Mars   1995   [E] — dc20   94-11181   CIP   AC

The artwork for each picture is an
ink drawing with watercolor painting.

"Hello, Beautiful!" whispered Max.

"I see you and I hear you, Max,"
said Max's sister, Ruby.

"And I see those lumps and bumps in your pajamas!"

"Back they go, Max," said Ruby. "One more of these
and you'll turn into a cupcake."

"Now, Max," said Ruby. "I am going to read you
   a bedtime story about someone whose sweet tooth got
   out of control. Are you ready, Max?"
"Yes!" said Max.
"Then listen up," said Ruby.

Once upon a time in Ancient Greece there was a little
prince named Midas who hated his fruits and vegetables.
Midas spent a lot of time in his mother's kitchen
glaring at her olive loaves. He kept trying to turn them
into sweets by developing laser-beam eyes.

One morning Midas's mother put prune whip on his melon.
"Oh, no," growled Midas.
"You must eat a good breakfast, my little pomegranate,"
    said his mother. "Then you will grow big and strong."

Midas decided to try something he had never done
before. As he laser-beamed his eyes, he whispered
the words "hot fudge sundae!" at the prune whip.
It worked beyond his wildest dreams.

Midas's breakfast was transformed into a table of
ice cream delights. Unfortunately his mother's hand
had gotten in the way of the laser-beam.
She became a cherry float.

The ice cream was delicious
and took until lunchtime to eat.

Midas's father called him into the fountain room for lunch.
"Spinach soup is full of vitamins, Son!" said Midas's dad.
Midas whispered the words "pistachio pop!" at the soup,
but just as he lasered his eyes at the spoon of green
liquid, he sneezed and nicked his father on the sleeve.

The spinach soup speedily turned into a pistachio pop,
but Midas's father was locked into the rubbery swirls
of a lime Jell-O surprise.

At four o'clock Midas's sister, Athena, called him
for an afternoon snack.

She had made him a freshly baked carrot muffin.
Aiming carefully, Midas zinged his laser eyes at the
muffin. But by accident he hiccuped, missed the muffin,
and ticked Athena on a whisker.

Athena became a slice of birthday cake.
Midas pleaded for her to come back, but no amount of
persuading could coax his sister out from the layers.

"What have I done?" moaned Midas.
He looked high and low for his family, but all he could
find was melted ice cream and sagging Jell-O.

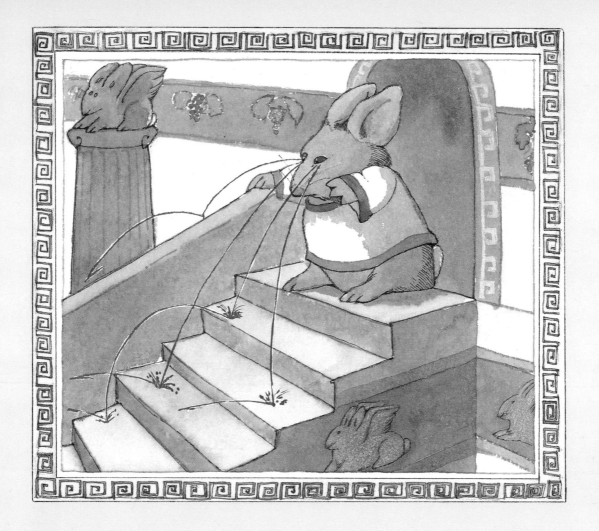

Midas sped to the top step of the escalarium. Using every volt
in his body, he sent his lasers scooting down the bannister, up the
drainpipes, and into every corner of every room in the house.
"Mom! Dad! Athena!" he shouted. "Come back!"
After a moment Midas heard tinkling laughter from the kitchen.

"Dinnertime!" said Midas's mother.
"And we have your favorite dessert for you!"
  said Midas's father.

"Hot fudge sundae!" Athena sang out.
"Oh, no," said Midas.

"Broccoli!" he whispered.

Ruby closed the book.
"Midas had too much of a good thing, didn't he, Max?"
asked Ruby.
But Max didn't answer.
"Good night, Max," said Ruby.

"Good night, Beautiful!" said Max.